CW00848471

A
J

First published in *More About Amelia Jane!* by Newnes 1954
This adaptation published by Egmont Books Limited 2003
239 Kensington High Street, London W8 6SA

Illustrations by Deborah Allwright

ISBN 1 4052 0530 X

1 3 5 7 9 10 8 6 4 2

Printed in Singapore.

A CIP catalogue record for this title is available from the British Library.

Enid Blyton™

Amelia Jane has a Clever Idea!

Illustrated by Deborah Allwright

EGMONT

One day, a small bear arrived at the nursery.
"I'm Sidney Gordon Eustace," he said proudly.
"I bet he gave himself that name," the clown said.
"No child would ever call a bear that name!"

"If you are staying," Amelia Jane told the bear, "then you have to do some chores like the rest of us."
"I don't want to," said Sidney bear, "so I won't!"
"Then you can't have any treats!" replied Amelia Jane.
The toys soon grew tired of lazy Sidney. If there was a job to be done, he was nowhere to be seen.
He never did any work at all!

"What shall we do about Sidney?" asked the big bear. "I know!" said Amelia Jane. "We will ask Sidney mouse to do Sidney bear's jobs! He won't like it when the mouse has the treats he could have had. He'll soon want to do the jobs himself, just you wait and see!"

"I didn't know the mouse is called Sidney," said Tom. "I just call 'mouse' at the mouse-hole and he comes!" "Well, I will call 'Sidney' and he'll still come," replied Amelia Jane. "Sidney!" she called. "Please help us!"

When the mouse appeared, Amelia Jane told him he could have a treat if he did some jobs for her. The mouse quickly did the things she wanted. "Isn't Sidney wonderful?" said Amelia Jane, loudly. "I mean Sidney mouse, not Sidney bear. Now here's that treat, Sidney, it's a tasty biscuit crumb!"

Sidney bear didn't like the toys calling the mouse Sidney. "Don't call that mouse again," he said. "I should be the only Sidney in the nursery!"

FIRE
FIRE

"Maybe the mouse's name is Sidney Gordon Eustace, just like you!" said Amelia Jane.
The bear didn't think a mouse could have the same grand name as him.

That night, the toys were having a party. Everyone helped get it ready, except Sidney bear.
"If you don't help, you can't come to the party!" said the big bear. But Sidney ignored him.

"I'll ask Sidney Gordon Eustace mouse to help us instead," said Amelia Jane.
"Sidney Gordon Eustace!" she called. "Please help us prepare for a party."

The bear couldn't believe it when the mouse appeared. Could it really be called Sidney Gordon Eustace, too? He watched jealously as the mouse did some jobs and was invited to the party. All the toys made a fuss of him.

"Thank you again for your help, Sidney Gordon Eustace," said Amelia Jane to the mouse at the end of the party. "Goodbye! See you soon!"

That was enough! The bear was fed up of the toys calling the mouse and giving it all his treats. He realised that if he did the jobs himself he could have the treats. He decided the next time there was a job to be done, he was going to do it! So when he heard Tom say the engine needed a

polish, the bear rushed over and cleaned it until it shone. And from then on, he did every job he was asked to do. He soon realised he liked being useful and the toys were all impressed with his hard work. Soon, they didn't call the mouse at all.

But one thing still puzzled Tom. "How did you know the mouse was called Sidney Gordon Eustace?" he asked Amelia Jane one day.
"It isn't!" she replied. "He will come if we call him

by any name because he knows he will get treats!" The big bear went to the mouse-hole. "Tomato soup!" he said. When the mouse appeared, he gave him a crumb. The toys all laughed.

Sidney bear was cross. He had been tricked! But as he looked around, he knew he wouldn't have all the friends he had now if Amelia Jane hadn't played her trick. The bear smiled. "What a clever idea!" he said and he laughed along with all the other toys.

A
J